Big Pumpkin

ERICA SILVERMAN

Illustrated by S. D. SCHINDLER

Aladdin Paperbacks

First Aladdin Paperbacks edition September 1995
Text copyright © 1992 by Erica Silverman
Illustrations copyright © 1992 by S. D. Schindler

Aladdin Paperbacks
An imprint of Simon & Schuster
Children's Publishing Division
1230 Avenue of the Americas
New York, NY 10020

Also available in a Simon & Schuster Books for Young Readers edition

The text of this book was set in 14-point Veljovic Medium.
The illustrations were done in gouache on colored paper.

Manufactured in China
30 29 28 27 26
The Library of Congress has cataloged the hardcover edition as follows:
Silverman, Erica.
Big pumpkin / Erica Silverman ; illustrated by S. D. Schindler. — 1st ed.   p.   cm.
Summary: A witch trying to pick a big pumpkin on Halloween discovers the
value of cooperation when she gets help from a series of monsters.
ISBN 978-0-02-782683-8
[1. Witches—Fiction. 2. Monsters—Fiction. 3. Pumpkin—Fiction.
4. Halloween—Fiction. 5. Cooperativeness—Fiction.]
I. Schindler, S. D., ill. II. Title.
PZ7.S58625Bi 1992
[E]—dc20 91-14053
ISBN 978-0-689-80129-7 (Aladdin pbk.)
0413 SCP

To Nicholas, Alexa, Jess, Sarah, Rafe,

Samantha, and Benjamin, with love

—E.S.

Once there was a witch who wanted to make pumpkin pie. So she planted a pumpkin seed. She weeded and watered, and after a while a sprout poked through. And then a pumpkin grew. And it grew. And it grew. And then it grew some more.

Soon Halloween was just hours away. The witch thought about pumpkin pie and bent down to take her pumpkin off the vine.

Well, she pulled and she tugged and she pulled. First she pulled hard and then she pulled harder. But that pumpkin just sat.

"Drat!" said the witch.

Just then, along came a ghost.

"Big pumpkin," said the ghost.

"It's big and it's mine, but it's stuck on the vine, and Halloween's just hours away," said the witch. And she kicked that pumpkin.

"I am bigger than you and stronger, too," boasted the ghost. "Let me try."

"Hmph!" said the witch. But she thought about pumpkin pie and stepped aside.

The ghost bent down to take the pumpkin off the vine.
Well, he pulled and he tugged and he pulled. First he pulled
hard and then he pulled harder. But that pumpkin just sat.
"Drat!" said the ghost.

Just then, along came a vampire.

"Big pumpkin," said the vampire.

"It's big and it's mine, but it's stuck on the vine, and Halloween's just hours away," said the witch. And she kicked that pumpkin.

"I am bigger than both of you and stronger, too," boasted the vampire. "Let me try."

"Hmph!" said the witch.

"Hmph!" said the ghost.

But they thought about pumpkin pie and stepped aside.
The vampire bent down to take the pumpkin off the vine.
Well, he pulled and he tugged and he pulled. First he
pulled hard and then he pulled harder. But that pumpkin
just sat.

"Drat!" said the vampire.

Just then, along came a mummy.

"Big pumpkin," said the mummy.

"It's big and it's mine, but it's stuck on the vine, and Halloween's just hours away," said the witch. And she kicked that pumpkin.

"I am bigger than all of you and stronger, too," boasted the mummy. "Let me try."

"Hmph!" said the witch.

"Hmph!" said the ghost.

"Hmph!" said the vampire.

But they thought about pumpkin pie and stepped aside.

The mummy bent down to take the pumpkin off the vine.

Well, she pulled and she tugged and she pulled. First she pulled hard and then she pulled harder. But that pumpkin just sat.

"Drat!" said the mummy.

Just then, along came a bat.

"Big pumpkin," said the bat.

The witch didn't say a word. She just looked at the ghost and rolled her eyes. The ghost looked at the vampire. The vampire looked at the mummy. They all looked at the little bat. And they started to laugh.

"I may not be big and I may not be strong," said the bat. "But I have an idea."

And the bat told them what to do.

"Hmph!" said the witch.

"Hmph!" said the ghost.

"Hmph!" said the vampire.

"Hmph!" said the mummy.

But they thought about pumpkin pie and bent down to take the pumpkin off the vine.

"Ready, set, pull!" called the bat.

The bat pulled the mummy, the mummy pulled the vampire, the vampire pulled the ghost, the ghost pulled the witch, and the witch pulled the pumpkin.

Well, they pulled and they tugged and they pulled. First they pulled hard and then they pulled harder. And...

Snap! Off came the pumpkin!
"Drat!" said the witch.
Whoosh! It flew and it flew and...

Thud! It landed on top of a hill and...
Thump-bump, thump-bump, thump-bump. It bounced
all the way down to the witch's house. And when it got to
her door, that pumpkin just sat.

"Hurray for the bat!" shouted the witch. And she hurried
inside to make pumpkin pie.

"Mmm," said the ghost.
"Have some more," said the witch.
"Couldn't eat another bite," said the vampire.
"Fun party," said the mummy.
"Time to go," said the bat.

"Drat!" said the witch as she watched them all leave.
Then she went right out and planted another pumpkin
seed.